D0065780

TRIP
D · A · Y

BY HARRIET ZIEFERT
ILLUSTRATED BY
RICHARD BROWN

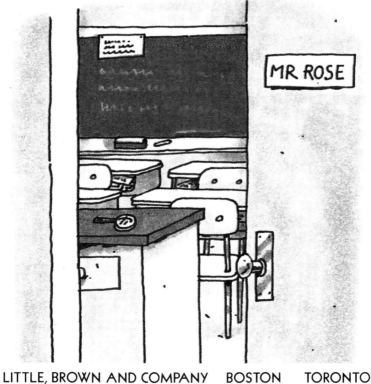

MR ROSE

LITTLE, BROWN AND COMPANY   BOSTON   TORONTO

First Edition

Library of Congress Cataloging-in-Publication Data
Ziefert, Harriet.
  Trip Day.

  (Mr. Rose series)
  [1. Pond ecology—Juvenile literature. I. Brown, Richard Eric,
1946-   ill. II. Title. III. Series.
QH541.5.P63Z44   1987   574.5'26322   86-2697
ISBN 0-316-98765-4

Published simultaneously in Canada
by Little, Brown & Company (Canada) Limited

Printed in Singapore for Harriet Ziefert, Inc.

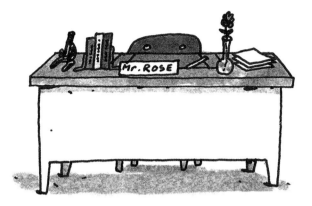

I remember all, but one, of my elementary
school teachers:
  Miss Kindervarder—Kindergarten
  Mrs. Sarasohn—Grade One
  Miss Pearl—Grade Two
            —Grade Three
  Mrs. Vork—Grade Four
  Mrs. Janpole—Grade Five
  Mr. Wolper—Grade Six
  Miss Benson—Grade Seven
  Miss Kelly—Grade Eight
  Miss Henderson—Music
  Mrs. Woelper—Art

CHAPTER ONE
TO THE POND

"Good morning, class! It's Wednesday,"
   said Mr. Rose.
"Good morning, Mr. Rose."
"Today we're going to begin learning about
   things that live in a pond. Is everyone
   ready for the field trip to the pond?"
   asked Mr. Rose.

"YEAH!" shouted the class.

"When do we leave?" asked Kelly, who
    couldn't wait to get going.

"We leave as soon as I'm sure everybody has
    what he needs," answered Mr. Rose. "Did
    you all remember plastic jars for collecting
    water samples?"

Everyone nodded yes, except Justin.

"Oops!" he moaned. "I forgot mine."

Kelly didn't want to be delayed.

"I brought three jars," she said. "I'll give
    you one."

"I remembered to wear old sneakers,"
    said Sarah.

"And I brought boots," said Sally.

"My mom says it's okay to get these clothes
    dirty," added Emily.

"Not *too* dirty, I hope," said Jennifer.

Jennifer liked to stay neat and clean.

She needed to be reminded getting dirty

was okay.

Sometimes.

Mr. Rose said, "It looks like everyone is ready.
Line up. The van is waiting. I'll carry
the two big, plastic buckets."
Everybody rushed to line up.
Kelly was first and Sarah was last.
As Mr. Rose was about to open the door,
Richard turned and yelled, "You jerk!
Watch it!"

"What's happening?" asked Mr. Rose.

"Justin was pushing. He stepped on my foot,"
Richard answered.

"But it was an accident!" Justin insisted.

Mr. Rose said, "Put the brakes on, Justin.
There's plenty of room in the van.
Let's go."

One by one the kids climbed into the van.
Adam asked for a front seat by the window
because he got car sick.
Richard and Matt took back seats.
They liked going over bumps.
Sarah and Sally sat together.
They had secrets to tell.
Kelly sat alone.
She didn't feel like talking.
She just wanted to get there.
Fast.
Emily sat across from Justin and Jamie.
And Jennifer sat next to Mr. Rose.
"Are all seat belts buckled?" the driver yelled.
Then he started the van.
On to the pond!

At first the van was pretty quiet.

No singing.

No yelling.

No arguing.

Just quiet talking.

And a few giggles from Sarah and Sally.

"Are we almost there?" Jennifer asked.

"Five more minutes," said Mr. Rose.

Justin looked over at Adam.

Adam looked funny—like he was about
to vomit.

Justin knew it would be disgusting
if Adam threw up.

"Mr. Rose, Adam looks sick!" he shouted.

Mr. Rose asked the driver to stop the van.

He took Adam outside and walked him around.

He told him to take deep breaths.

"Adam's a wimp," whispered Justin.

"No, he's not!" Sarah said. "He's trying not
    to get sick."

Adam and Mr. Rose got back on the van.

"Feeling better?" Mr. Rose asked.

"A little," said Adam, as the driver
    started up the van.

Pretty soon Mr. Rose said, "We're here!"

"Finally," said Adam, who looked as
    green as his shirt.

It was a beautiful spring day.

Birds chirped.

Insects buzzed.

The sun shone.

A perfect day for a field trip!

The pond was big, but shallow.

Mr. Rose called everyone together
at the water's edge.

"Can anyone tell me why we're here?"
Mr. Rose asked.

"So we can learn about pond animals,"
said Jennifer.

"Right," said Mr. Rose. "And to do it,
we need to collect water and a lot of mud."

"Mud?" Jennifer asked, wrinkling her nose
as if she smelled something bad.

"Yes—mud!" said Mr. Rose. "And when
you see water plants, get them too. But
don't put land plants in your jars.
They will rot."

"How about green scum?" Emily asked,
    pointing to a clump floating on
    the water. "Should we get that
    stuff too?"
"Definitely!" Mr. Rose answered. "The scum
    is algae. Scoop up as much as you can."
"YEECH!" said Jennifer.
"How about sticks?"
"And stones?"
"Get them, too," answered Mr. Rose.
    "Because tiny microscopic animals cling
    to sticks and stones."
"What if they're too big for the jar?"
    Sarah asked.
"Bring them to me," Mr. Rose said.
    "I'll show you what to do. And
    don't collect any large animals like turtles.
    They're too big to live in our small aquarium
    at school. All set? Any more questions?"
There were no more questions.
Everybody was anxious to begin.
Collecting time had finally come.

Jennifer, Justin, and Kelly
walked off together.
"I hope I see a frog," Andrew said.
"Me too!" said Kelly.
"I bet you don't know the difference between
    a frog and a toad," said Jennifer.
"What makes you so smart?" Justin teased.
"I'm smart because I read. I read a book
    about frogs and toads—and tadpoles, too."
"Don't tell me about it," said Kelly. "I want
    to find out for myself!"
Just then something splashed.
Kerplop!
Was it a frog?
A toad?
Only Jennifer knew.

CHAPTER TWO
LOOK WHAT WE FOUND

Sally waded toward the middle of the pond.

She bent over and put her hand into the water.

She reached all the way down.

She felt mud.

Mushy, squishy mud.

Sally grabbed a handful and plopped it
into her jar.

Sally held up her jar.

"Is this enough mud?" she asked Mr. Rose.

"How about one more handful," he answered.

"Mud from the middle is just what we need."

"Mr. Rose!" shouted Emily. "I found
a big stick—too big for my jar. And it has
slimy stuff on it. Lots."

"Come over here," said Mr. Rose. "I'll help you."

Mr. Rose held the stick over the jar.

He showed Emily how to rinse the algae and
tiny animals off and flush them into the jar.

Richard put a jar of pond water right under
Justin's nose.

"Smell this," he said.

Justin took a big whiff.

Sniff! Sniff!

"It smells okay," he said, as he wiped his nose.

Mr. Rose said, "A healthy pond doesn't smell."

"What's a healthy pond?" asked Sarah.

"I've never heard of a healthy pond—
or a sick one, either."

Mr. Rose answered, "When we get back
to school and take out the magnifying lenses
and the microscope, you'll see what I mean
by a healthy pond."

"Wow!" said Kelly. "A real microscope! Can
I be the first to look through the lens?"

"You'll all take turns," answered Mr. Rose.

"I'm not making any promises about
who will be first."

"Can we drink this water?" Richard asked.

"Probably, yes," said Mr. Rose. "But it's not
a good idea to drink from a pond unless
you see a sign that says: *Safe for Drinking.*"

"But I'm thirsty," Richard complained.

"We'll be having juice and cookies soon,"
said Mr. Rose.

"Snack time is so boring!" said Matt.
"We always have the same stuff."

"We could have worms," said Jennifer.

"Or frogs' legs."

"Or snails."

"Or pony tails!" said Richard, as he pulled on
Jennifer's hair and pretended to eat it.

"Get away!" yelled Jennifer,
giving Richard a shove.

"By snack time I'll be so hungry, I'll eat anything!"
said Emily with a giggle.

"And I'm so thirsty, I could drink this whole
pond," grumbled Richard.

All of a sudden there was a big splash.

It wasn't a frog...

or a stick...

or a rock...

or a branch...

It was Justin!

Justin had slipped and fallen into the pond.

All the kids laughed.

Mr. Rose asked, "Justin, are you all right?"

"I'm okay," he answered, trying not to cry.

Mr. Rose gave Justin a towel.

"Were you trying to test the water for Richard?"
he kidded.

Justin smiled a little.

Then Mr. Rose said, "Don't worry. The sun
will dry you pretty fast."

Everybody was so busy watching Justin that
they didn't notice what Richard was doing.
Richard found something—something good.
He hid it in his pocket.
He wanted to keep it a secret.
A secret for later.
A secret for the classroom.
A secret for Sally.

"Okay, time to stop!" Mr. Rose shouted.

"Everyone come over here and sit down."

"Do we *have* to stop?" asked Emily.

"Yes," said Mr. Rose. "I think we have enough samples of pond water."

Mr. Rose continued, "What else do we have?"

Everyone shouted their answers.

"SNAILS!"

"GREEN SCUM!"

"WATER BUGS!"

"PLANTS!"

"MUD!"

"STICKS!"

"Does anybody have anything else?"
Mr. Rose asked.

No one answered.

Not Richard, nor anyone else.

Then Mr. Rose said, "I'll bet that when we
get back and start looking closely
at the pond water—with magnifying lenses—
you'll find at least a hundred animals!"

"He must be kidding!" Emily said.

"Maybe not," said Sarah.

A hundred animals—alive in the pond water.

That was hard to believe.

29

"Do you really think I'll find anything in this
    jar?" Justin asked Jamie as they rode
    back to school.
"Maybe you'll find a bunch of weird beasties,"
    Jamie answered.
"I wish I had a magnifying lens right now,"
    said Justin.
"Me, too," Jamie said. "A lens makes tiny things
    a hundred times bigger. Right?"
  Mr. Rose leaned over.
"I'll give you a clue," he said. "Once we get back
    to school, check the handle of the lens
    I give you."
"Okay," said Jamie.

CHAPTER THREE
IN A DROP OF WATER

"Now we're going to find out what's hiding
in the water and mud," announced Mr. Rose.
He stood at a big table near the window.
Everyone watched as he poured the mud and
water from his buckets into the aquarium.
"This aquarium is for the whole class," he said.
Then he pointed to lots of good stuff
on the table.

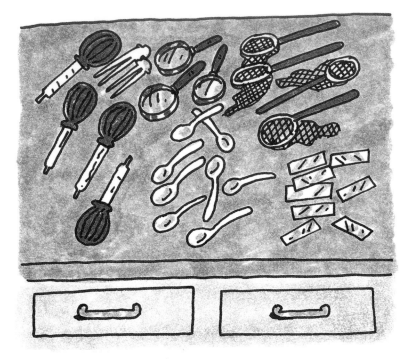

There were hand magnifying glasses—
enough for everybody.
Big eyedroppers with black rubber squeezers.
Lots of glass slides.
Plastic spoons.
Nets.
Good stuff, all of it.

Mr. Rose demonstrated how to suck up
a dropperful of pond water, then squeeze it
onto a glass slide.
He gave everyone an eyedropper and two slides
and said, "Try it!"
"This will be a cinch!" said Justin.
But he was in for a big surprise—eyedroppers
weren't always so easy to use.
Sometimes Justin would squeeze OUT
when he wanted to pull IN.
Sometimes he pulled IN
when he wanted to squeeze OUT.

Justin put a drop of water on the slide.
He chose a magnifying lens and
checked the handle. It said, "Ten power."
"What's it mean?" he asked Mr. Rose.
Mr. Rose answered, "A ten-power lens makes
everything ten times bigger."
Now Justin was ready to start looking.
At first he didn't see anything.
Then he shouted, "There's something here
with lots and lots of legs!"
Justin showed it to Sarah and Sally.
Mr. Rose said, "Why don't the three of you
make drawings of the animal Justin found?"
"We will," Sarah answered.
"I like to draw beasts," said Sally.
"Even weird ones."

Matt and Richard were sharing the
one-hundred-power microscope.
It was hard to focus.
It took a long time to find anything.
"Let me try," Emily said.
"Good luck," said Matt. "It isn't easy."
"Look!" said Emily. "Here's one with huge eyes!"
"Let me see!" yelled Richard.
"Me, too!" shouted Matt.
"What is it?" Emily asked Mr. Rose.
"I'm not telling."
"Please..." Emily begged.
"No," said Mr. Rose. "Right now the name
    is not important. It's more important
    that you learn how to look.
    And learn how to find out."
"You mean we have to find out about these
    animals for ourselves," said Richard.
"That's what I mean," said Mr. Rose.
"But that's hard," said Matt.
"But worth it," said Mr. Rose.

Everybody drew pictures.

Mr. Rose said the pictures were important.
"It's good to remember what you see with
a picture," he said. "And good to see
how your picture is the same or different
from someone else's."

Emily and Adam drew animals with many legs.

Jamie's creature had one big eye.

Justin drew a tadpole like this:

And Jennifer and Kelly drew snails.

Sarah and Sally were observing two snails.

"They leave trails of goo!" noticed Sarah.

"And slide slowly!" added Sally.

Sarah and Sally decided to set up a snail race.

"We need a track," said Sarah.

"How should we make it?" Sally asked.

"We can cut a piece of cardboard and make
a racing strip."

"Should we wet it?"

"I think so," said Sarah. "I think the snails
will slide better if the track is wet."

"But how do you know?"

"I don't," Sarah answered.

"Then you're just guessing," said Sally.

"Not exactly," answered Sarah. "Water
on a track is like snail goo. It should help
the snails to slide better. And go faster."

Mr. Rose overheard the conversation.

"You're on the right track, Sarah," he said.

"To test your idea, you should really make
two tracks—one wet, and one dry. And
by the way, how do you know a pond snail
will move at all when it's out of the water?"

"We don't," the girls answered.

"Well," said Mr. Rose, "why don't you try to
find out and then tell everybody else
what you learned."

"Okay," said Sarah. "We'll try."

"Class, I have an announcement," said Mr. Rose.
"Sarah and Sally are experimenting to
find out how snails move. You all should
be watching the ways the animals you've
found move. Do they wiggle? Do they spin?
Do they swim in straight lines?"
"I'll show you how one moves," said Jamie.
Jamie stood in the center of the classroom.
Everyone watched as she spun around
just like a whirligig beetle.
"That looks like fun," said Emily.
"Can I try?"
"Me too!"
"I have an idea," said Mr. Rose. "Let's all
do 'weird beastie dances' at recess.
I'll put on music and we can all move
like the tiny animals we've been observing."

EMILY

Richard walked to Sally's and Sarah's table.
"What are you doing?" he asked.
"You heard Mr. Rose," answered Sally.
  "We're experimenting."
"And we're going to have a snail race,"
  Sarah added.
  Richard thought, "It's going to be a slow race,
    unless…"
  Richard smiled to himself.
"Unless I liven things up."
  Richard knew what he would do.
  Soon.
  Very soon he would do it.

CHAPTER FOUR
BEAST ON THE LOOSE

Emily rested her eye on the black
eyepiece of the microscope.
"Wow!" she yelled. "I see a whole bunch
   of little white things!"
Matt said, "If your drop of water has a whole
   bunch of things, and if my drop has a
   whole bunch, then Mr. Rose was right.
   There are hundreds of tiny animals
   in this classroom right now!"

"Matt's crazy," Justin said.

"Matt's not crazy," said Mr. Rose. "He's
    thinking. He's drawing conclusions
    based on what he's seen."

Emily was thinking too. She said, "If I knew
    how many drops of water there were in that
    aquarium, and if I knew how many animals
    were in each drop, then I could multiply to
    find out how many there are altogether."

"You don't know how to multiply such
    big numbers!" said Adam.

"So, I'll use a calculator or a computer,"
    answered Emily.

"But how do you know there are the same number
    of tiny animals in each drop?" Adam asked.

"I don't," Emily said.

"So, you can't do it!"

"Well, maybe I can't," said Emily. "But I can
    still think about it."

Emily remembered Mr. Rose had said that
    thinking was good—even when you can't
    figure out an answer.

Questions were good, too.

Kelly asked, "Do you think there are dead
animals in that aquarium?"

"If we have live ones, I suppose we have
dead ones," Emily answered.

"Not too many, I hope," added Kelly.

"If we had too many, our aquarium would stink,"
Jennifer said. "Dead things smell bad.
Like old garbage. Yuck!"

"Maybe that's what Mr. Rose meant when he said
a healthy pond doesn't smell," said Kelly.

"Good thinking, Kelly," said Mr. Rose, as
he walked by.

Something was moving in Richard's pocket.
Richard touched it and knew it was still alive.
He walked over to Sally.
She was watching her snail move very slowly
along a wet track.
Sarah was reading to Sally from a book:

> *Your snail has two pairs of horns.*
> *Can you see them? The front two are*
> *for feeling its way and the back two*
> *have eyes on the end. Remember, when*
> *your snail is frightened, it hides*
> *its horns.*

Neither Sarah nor Sally paid any attention
to Richard.
He reached into his pocket.
He pulled something out and quickly put it
on the table.
Then he walked away.

49

Almost immediately, that something moved.
Jump! Jump!
Sarah dropped the book on the floor!
The snail hid its horns!
And Sally shrieked:
  "EEK! A FROG!
    A REAL LIVE FROG!"

"Mr. Rose! Mr. Rose! There's a
    beast on the loose!"
"Catch it! Catch it!"
"But it's slippery!"
"It's jumpy!"
"It's scared!"

The frog jumped all over.
At least five kids were running after it.
Mr. Rose shouted, "EVERYBODY FREEZE!"
From the sound of his voice everyone knew
Mr. Rose really meant it.

Mr. Rose tiptoed quietly behind the frog.

He reached out quickly and grabbed it.

Someone clapped.

But Mr. Rose looked upset.

He held the frog in his cupped hands and asked,
"Who brought this back from the pond?"

There was no answer.

Mr. Rose repeated the question.

Again no answer.

"I said we couldn't keep large animals alive
in our classroom aquarium," said Mr. Rose.

Richard felt ashamed.

He said, "I'm the one who did it."

"You're mean!" said Sally. "And you ruined
our snail race!"

"The race can continue tomorrow," said
Mr. Rose. "Right now I want everybody
back in his own seat."

Richard said he was sorry for upsetting everybody.

And the frog, too.

Mr. Rose put the frog in a small aquarium.
It would not be easy to keep a single frog
alive in there for long.
He said, "I'll take it back to the pond
on my way home from school."
Then Mr. Rose looked at the clock.
He told everybody it was clean-up time.
"Pond water jars should be left uncovered
on the window sill," he said. "We'll
be using them again."
Then Mr. Rose wrote a question on the board:
How can we tell if something is alive?
"It moves," said Justin.
"What else?"
"It eats," answered Jennifer.
"Anything else?" asked Mr. Rose.
"It grows," said Kelly.
Mr. Rose was pleased.
He said "You know how to think. You can
figure things out for yourselves."
"Hooray for us!" shouted Justin.

"Can pond animals think?" asked Emily.

"Hooray for Emily," said Mr. Rose.

"That's a good question."

"What's the answer?" Jennifer asked.

"I'm not telling," said Mr. Rose.

"I want some other good questions first."

Everybody started shouting at once.

"Wait a minute!" said Mr. Rose. "Raise
    your hands, please."

One by one, Mr. Rose added more questions
to the blackboard:

Where do tiny animals come from?

Do pond-water animals sleep?

Do they have bones? Blood?

What do pond-water animals eat?

Do they breathe?

Could pond animals live in the ocean?

Could they live in water from the sink?

How long do they live?

What happens to the animals when they die?

59

"Do we have to figure out the answers
     to all these questions?" asked Jennifer.
"Not today," said Mr. Rose. "We'll save them
     on the blackboard until we've studied
     more about plants and animals. But what
     did we figure out today?"
"A lot of animals live in pond water," said Matt.
"In *healthy* pond water," added Kelly.
  Sally said, "They all look different."
"And wiggle differently," said Jamie.
"Good," said Mr. Rose. "What else?"
"Snails can move outside of pond water,"
     said Sarah.
"But we still don't know if a wet or dry track
     is fastest," Sally complained,
     glaring at Richard.
"But you did learn how to set up an
     experiment," Mr. Rose said. "And Richard
     learned something, too."
"Large animals should stay in the pond,"
     said Richard.
"Right!"

"What are we going to do tomorrow?"
Matt asked.
"I have a good idea," said Mr. Rose.
"But I'd rather keep it to myself."
"Please tell," Jennifer begged.
"You can wait," answered Mr. Rose. "You
can wait until tomorrow. See you
Thursday. Class dismissed."

Homework

- Go outside, find a hundred of something, then prove it.

- Collect a hundred of something

Express
- ~~express~~ your feelings about "a hundred" in 50 words or less.

Have fun!
Mr. Rose